We Help Mommy

BY JEAN CUSHMAN

PICTURES BY ELOISE WILKIN

A GOLDEN BOOK, New York
Western Publishing Company, Inc.
Racine, Wisconsin 53404

FOR MARTHA AND BOBBY CUSHMAN, HOLLY REED AND LARRY O'LOANE

Before Jean Cushman became Mrs. Cushman, she was Jean Burger, and she helped to make many Golden Books. Now the publishers are happy to be able to present Jean's own book about her children, Martha and Bobby, who spend the day "helping Mommy." The pictures are by Eloise Wilkin, who asked two young friends, Holly Reed and Larry O'Loane, to pose for the delightful pictures.

We help Mommy every day.
We help her in the morning, as soon as we get up.
We take off our pajamas.

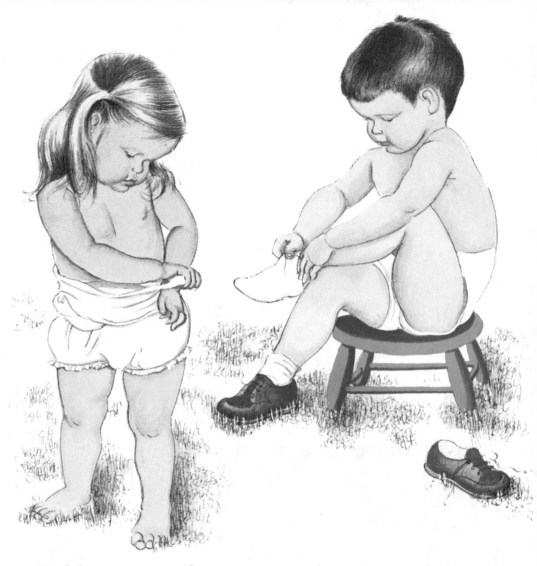

Bobby puts on his pants, and socks, and shoes.
He can dress himself. I put on mine.
Over my head goes my shirt.
Oops! My arm is stuck.
Mommy will help me pull it out.

Mommy buckles my shoes.
"You're a good girl, Martha," says Mommy.
"You can almost dress yourself."

We all go down for breakfast.
Bobby breaks the eggs for Daddy to fry.
I put bread in the toaster.
Out it pops, hot and brown!
"You two are a big help," says Daddy.

We wave good-by to Daddy from the door.
Then it's time to make Mommy's bed.
"Pull the sheet tight," Mommy says.
We pull until there's not a wrinkle left.
"Thank you," says Mommy when we're done.

Swish! swish! goes the broom.
Pfuff! pfuff! goes the dust mop.
Brr! brr! goes the carpet sweeper
as it picks up the dirt.

We are cleaning house.
Under the beds, over the rugs,
in all the corners we clean.
"Here is a dustcloth for you," says Mommy.
Bobby dusts the table-tops
while I mop under the chairs.

Now it's time to wash.
We collect the clothes.
Bobby puts Daddy's clothes
   in the washing machine.
I put my dolly's clothes in.

In goes the soap.
Bang! goes the door.
Hmmmmm! goes the machine.
Round and round the clothes go.
I can see my face in the shiny glass.

My clothesline isn't high like Mommy's.
It is just right for me.
I hang up dolly's clothes.
Two clothespins for her dress.
One clothespin for each sock.
And one clothespin for her hat.

We see Ann and Jerry playing
in their sandbox next door.
"Come on over, Martha and Bobby!" they call.
"Run along," says Mommy.
"Take your pails and shovels.
Have fun!"

Once a week we go to the supermarket.
I ride in the cart while Bobby pushes.
Up and down the aisles we go.
"What would you like today?" asks Mommy.

We tell her cereal and apples
and cookies and raisins and a picture book.
We pile them on the counter.
Mommy has two big bags
and Bobby and I have little bags to carry home.

We like to put things away for Mommy.
The cereal goes in the cabinet,
the apples in the basket,
the cookies and raisins on the shelf.
"You're a big help," says Mommy.

Soon it is time for lunch.
Mommy gets the bread and cheese and meat.
I spread butter on two slices.
Bobby puts meat and cheese on two others.
Slap! Mommy puts them together.
What yummy sandwiches!

Now we set the table.

A place mat for Mommy.
And place mats for Bobby and me.
A knife and fork for Mommy.
A fork for each of us.
Napkins for us all.

After lunch Mommy washes the dishes.
She lets me dry the forks and spoons.
"Here's a spoon for you, Martha."
I take it from the dish rack
and rub it all over gently.
Bobby puts the dishes away.

I sit on a stool when I help Mommy bake pies.
Mommy mixes the dough in a big bowl.
She gives me a little ball of dough
to make a treat for Daddy.

Roll, pat. Roll, pat.
I'm making a treat for Daddy.
It's a funny man, with two cherries for eyes,
and one cherry for a mouth.
"Daddy will be very pleased," says Mommy.
And she puts it in the oven.

We've had a busy day helping Mommy.
Soon it is time to put away our toys
and books and clothes and get ready for bed.

We sing our put-away song:
In the box we put the blocks,
The dolls go in the crib;
Teddy Bear sits on the chair—
Puts on his bright blue bib.

Daddy comes to say good-night and tuck me in.
"That was a delicious treat, Martha," he says.
"Thank you both for being such a big help
to Mommy and me.
Sleep tight."